A Child of World War II Writes:

LOVE IS TIMELESS IN WAR AND IN PEACE: A TRUTH BEYOND COMPARE

Lourdes J. Astraquillo Ongkeko, Ph.D.

A Child of World War II Writes:
Love is Timeless in War and in Peace:
A Truth Beyond Compare
by Lourdes J. Astraquillo Ongkeko, Ph.D.

ISBN 978-1-970072-47-1 (Paperback)
ISBN 978-1-970072-48-8 (Hardback)

Printed in the United States of America.

New Leaf Media, LLC
175 S. 3rd Street, Suite 200
Columbus, OH 43215
www.thenewleafmedia.com

Foreword

A 13-year old youngster's story focuses on the 4-year War in the Pacific, a major chapter of World War II that started with the bombing of her hometown, Baguio City, Island of Luzon, Northern Philippines, on December 8, 1941. When the enemy forces arrived that same day, bombs fell close to the public high school where she was enrolled as a sophomore.

The story, told by the same child of war, the Philippine Campaign, has kept its place in history: it tells how numbers of the Filipino youth fared during that period described as one of the largest joint campaigns of the Pacific phase of World War II.

It details a huge part of the Filipino youth: how their hopes and the return of freedom to that former colony of the United States of America were never extinguished.

A thirteen-year old youngster then, now a mother of three; grandmother of six; and great grandmother of seven, has marked reminiscences on the four-year War in the Pacific, a major chapter of World War II that started with the carpet bombing of her hometown, Baguio City, Island of Luzon, Northern Philippines, on December 8, 1941.

When the enemy forces arrived that same day, bombs fell close to the public high school where she was enrolled as a sophomore. Not a single individual had any knowledge about bombing. Since that eventual date, survival through prayer became the goal of all survivors. Coping with the invaders, became a central part of their lives. But they never lost track that liberty would return as enshrined in their hearts knowing the moment of liberation would come.

Love is Timeless in War and in Peace: A Truth Beyond Compare

During times of strife, there are certain emotions that are severely tried. Standing out on its own, is love. It can be defined in many ways, but it can likewise prove how it is strongly tested in war and in peace.

The author, at the tender age of thirteen (13) found boundless and unceasing love from her father who patiently monitored what their family had to face abruptly as several aspects of war surfaced without notice at all.

She said:

"My father emphasized on holding our own as a family unit. We were to let him know what we immediately needed in terms of nourishment. If we felt unwell, he should be the first to receive the information. We, who were the immediate recipients of his caring attitude and love drew much knowledge relevant to dealing with certain cultural differences exhibited by the enemy forces when time was of the essence."

The word "war" is enough to make anyone shudder. Yet, memories return. Details surface. They are meant to act as reminders: As precious as life itself.

I am a child of war. World War II made its first appearance when my old hometown, the city of Baguio, in Northern Philippines, was part of the major invasion by the Japanese armed forces. When December 8, 1941 arrived on the scene, I was in high school as a first-semester sophomore. Not one could tell war had just commenced. Nobody knew about the definition of war. It was a phenomenon. Visualized on screen, by three movie houses in the heart of the city; the news stories' portrayal was the closest understanding cinema goers could relate to. World War I scenes as seen through the European theaters of war were viewed intermittently.

That day in December, strong explosions suddenly came after one another. They were so loud that everyone who heard them thought all of us on that same high school campus were going to lose the facility of hearing. Nobody could figure out where the almost-deafening noises came from. Tears blurred our eyesight. We simply could not determine how we would continue to cover our ears to prevent us from listening to the almost non-stop blasts. Instead, five of us, school-mates who lived within walking distance to one another, sought each other, as we clung to any post we could lean on. Peace of mind was making its departure as the clear air substituted by smoke, made us cough intensely.

More and more shouts filled the air; explosions were identified as coming from articles blown in mid-air.

Some parts fell on the ground. There was an intense fear that fire would break out wherever those same particles landed. Heavy smoke looked like it blanketed the same grounds we were running away from.

All we were told to do by our teachers' frantic instructions was for us to go home as fast as we could. We had to leave the scene because we were tragically informed how nobody could protect us. We could scarcely hear one another. Loud explosions continued to fill the air. So did black, threatening dark clouds as though they would just land on us. The skies above us suddenly turned gray. The early sunlight was gulfed into a giant dismal blanket that turned light into dark instantly.

As a first-semester sophomore, rules were rules. All we were told to "obey" was repeated as a formidable command: "Go home as fast as you can. Have your name tags on."

Certain initial explosions arrived some few miles away from our high school grounds. Our ears failed to fend off the loud noises which were unknown to us. They were growing in volume. They seemed so close to us as we heard them explode simultaneously. We failed to hear calm voices. We heard loud cries only. Loud shouts. Louder shrieks. More and more shouts for assistance came from all over. Mixed with loud rumbles exploding from the items dropping briskly from the airplanes, all kinds of disturbing noise were subject to exercises in guessing. Chief among the guessing category was to determine where they came from.

Ceaseless shouts mixed with piercing cries were heard. So many loud calls came from all over our high school's huge building! Not one set of instructions could be followed. It was total confusion that reigned alone. We failed to recognize where numbers of students were headed for. Absolutely, nobody could tell us what direction to take.

Nobody knew what was going to happen next. All of a sudden, the five of us found ourselves alone. We had to walk home. Some of my classmates left their books on the school grounds. I didn't. In fact, since it was but a couple of hours after our flag ceremony of December 8, 1941, I was able to go ahead to my classroom. Before we left our campus, I hurriedly gathered all my books and notebooks. Truly, whatever I could carry by myself was all that mattered at the moment. Books couldn't just be shunted aside. I instantly recalled how my father, since he taught me how to read, informed us about the invaluable role of books in one's lifetime. I looked for manila paper to protect the books I carried.

What was heard from the school's loudspeaker was clear: "Go home. If you hear sounds like you did during the first explosions traced to Camp John Hay (a facility just a couple of miles away from our Baguio City High School), seek shelter immediately. Go to a place where you can have protection. A roof that will cover you will do."

We walked as fast as we could. In fact, we ran just as we could shield ourselves from the incessant noise that came from the items falling from the sky as they grew in number and intensity.

What usually took half-an-hour in walking became much longer because we paid attention to other explosions that were taking place around our beloved lovely city, way, one locale we loved beyond any comparison.

Young as we were, we cried endlessly. We had no idea that war had just announced itself. We thought the object of the articles falling from the sky had met their fate. Silence came. It lasted only a half-hour. Then another similar set of non-stop explosions took place. We were now convinced we might die anytime. We never, never had any inkling about war; not one among the school population knew the reality that war had arrived at our front door that fast; we started to talk to ourselves: where was the back door that would spirit us out of the miles closest to safety?

Yet, another series of explosions whose noise volumes were now familiar to us came from more and more explosions taking place simultaneously.

As we hurriedly left our high school grounds, we tried to scamper for shelter. Any roof would do as long as we didn't see those dreadful things falling down from the sky.

Much later, three elders we met on our "escape" route informed us that those items dropping from the sky were huge bombs; as they exploded, their mission was ful- filled: they had struck the U.S.- owned famous fort. From a short distance, we decided to proceed to the most well-kept area called Camp John Hay. Even from hundreds of feet away, the large buildings were covered by black soot. The once- lovely gardens surrounding the camp were overflowing with dust. Large bits of burnt items that had the most unknown smell filling the air joined the atmosphere we were now getting accustomed to, as short breathing spells laced with sad cries came from the five of us.

Many floral gardens were aflame. Their colorful petals no longer could be distinguished from one another. They were all flying around the same air we were breathing. Dust. Smoke. The harsh smell of burning twigs likewise became too strong. We were afraid we could no longer breathe. We noticed how the same smoke that was turning black grew thicker and thicker.

We, who started to walk home, cried as loud as we could together. We loved our city. We started to recall how it stood among other sister cities in the Philippines. We tried to sing to stop us from weeping so loudly as though our chests would break. But our cries surpassed any melodies and tunes that we could no longer sing.

Mourning loudly seemed to help us forget our tribulations. Our fears. Our sense of loss. Our unknown anxieties piling in number. Although we were public school students, we were all Catholics. We didn't have our rosaries with us. But we remembered our prayers. We all prayed together, as loudly as we could. Praying together stopped us from crying loudly. Tears were shed almost incessantly as we repeatedly prayed.

Baguio, without any hint of contradiction, was considered the most beautiful city shining among all island gems that constituted the Philippine archipelago.

We, who identified Baguio as home, were proud to be called "sons and daughters of Baguio."

Although a great many among us, whose parents came from several points in the country spoke several dialects, we all settled on English, our sole medium of conversation. Numbers among us weren't even at nodding acquaintance with their parents' original dialects.

It wasn't uncommon among us to converse in English because there were some ten (10) dialects that were spoken by other households. It was simpler to adhere to English. The language became our bond.

Aside from being a geographical spot that stood clearly as one of Mother Nature's favorites, Baguio stood unparalleled in its singular loveliness and clean air that sprung from its lofty location: five thousand feet: yes, 5,000 feet above sea level, truly way beyond any other site that numerous members of the country's populace could draw reasonable comparisons. Although our country received the name, "Pearl of the Orient Seas," we enjoyed hearing how Baguio was considered a prized jewel, veritably so described: Beyond compare.

We, who were identified as Baguio youngsters tried to prove to the best of our abilities that we would strive hard in school to make our city proud of us, achievement-wise.

It was not infrequent when the student body would be informed by our teachers that they were prone to submitting students' names as candidates to various academic contests; fortunately, Baguio's representatives did not fail. Student leaders deserved their titles. We, their younger sisters, referred to them for guidance.

Competition meant to represent our high school, thus our beloved city as well, became so popular and synonymous with triumph.

Our teachers trained us to run away with major prizes coming from contests where provincial meets were held in various parts of our Ilocos region.

Those who were identified as representatives of Baguio won handily top national prizes in contests that involved simple mathematical knowledge expected from their grade placement; oratorical contests, all in English, some authored by the participants themselves and choral music ensembles that tested natural vocal contestants and their musical instrument players that could vie with other performers as students of learning, were not uncommon triumphs.

Baguio, as we youngsters had noted, inspired us no end in providing inspiration that would lead us to reach the many futures ahead. We leaned on our humble successful attempts at achievements as long as we adhered to the rules of discipline that anchored us in our quest for the goals of education.

How World War II truly arrived as fast as we heard airplanes amid our city's skyline was totally unknown to us as we ran toward all streets that would lead us home.

We ran briskly to the sole public areas we believed were open: the City Market, food supply sources, some stores we knew sold nourishing offerings manned by the natives and residents of Baguio. In our intense disappointment, all were draped in heavy boards and extra-thick canvas covers. We had hoped to find some refreshments and water to drink.

As we continued to find our way home, we did not come across any adult who could be aware at all that war was real. Fear was no longer in doubt. We didn't have to be convinced that we were endangered.

Airplanes were still in flight as their sight dotted our city's skyline. The skies continued to remain dark.

In a couple of hours, after we were able to avoid the main roads and busy streets, the five of us who started our trek from our high school grounds, scampered to our respective homes. Three from our group were juniors and seniors, but since we grew up together, the age difference didn't matter at all.

Teary-eyed, we hugged one another, assuring each other that we would continue to keep in touch as we were wont to doing.

I climbed the lengthy stairs of our three-story residence. My parents were awaiting word from all of us, their four children who attended different schools. Since I was the one who came from the farthest point of the city, I was the last one who joined the family. My father hurriedly left his office as soon as the initial news hit the city so he could assuage my expectant mother who didn't stop weeping. She was due still in 1942. Papa was concerned they would have a pre-mature baby, as the turmoil grew rapidly around the city. Pharmacies were closed. Ditto doctors' clinics. No first-aid shelters were open.

Papa gathered all of us, his four schoolchildren. He informed us clearly how he had to construct an air-raid shelter on our compound immediately. Not knowing how that shelter would look like, all of us eagerly awaited answers to our many queries. Papa brought out the plan he had agreed upon with the workers. The shelter would be high enough to allow us to seek refuge where mattresses would cover the floor. Looking at the plan, it did look like a cave. There was but one entrance. It was supposed to be disguised with trees and low shrubs.

What Papa underscored was how the shelter would allow us to store canned goods. We were youngsters, we had no idea about what was to ensue. How could we all be accommodated in such a place, was a query that didn't escape us. Can we sleep in that shelter? Or, would we just occupy the shelter when bombs that we'd seen in air were no longer dropping from the airplanes?

As soon as darkness appeared, four men started the work on the shelter. It took them more than eight (8) hours to finish the job, way into the night and early dawn, so quietly, as they concentrated on the details they read by the dim light coming from lamps. Steel posts were visible inside. A lamp that relied on batteries was to provide light for the shelter's interior. The floor was covered by layers of thin mats. Very thin mattresses lined the shelter's walls. Benches that could suffice for us youngsters to lie on, were covered with blankets.

No footwear was allowed at all for all occupants of the shelter. The last job was to cover the entrance with pine trees and nobody but the workers and our family could ever identify the shelter at all. Fortunately, there was a spring in our vicinity. Water was not a problem. Besides, we had vegetable gardens that started to provide us with fresh salads. Our fruit trees appeared just right for the picking.

In twenty-four (24) hours, the main road to our neighborhood changed abruptly. Principal streets sprung a new look. Sentry posts and high walls leading to the main roads that had to be traversed, were immediately installed. Recorded warnings were repeated instantly. The "or-else" part of the calls for complete compliance metamorphosed at once. Guardhouses exhibited and exposed their weapons as sentries stood by. We were informed that sentries occupied all main streets although, but a hundred feet apart, close enough to be in full view of one another.

Since sentries were all over the city, all pedestrians who would walk by them, had to bow correctly as subjects were expected to obey. Initially, we learned how one sentry demonstrated the "bow."

Bowing was not just a shallow one. It had to be in compliance with what the authorities demonstrated: deep enough; too, pedestrians were not to leave the sentry site unless cleared to depart.

Bowing at every sentry where there were soldiers, became a common sight. Our elders failed to bow as deeply as they were told. Those who failed to follow instructions were whipped: Beaten by ropes tied to thick sticks. They were not allowed to get up until they could repeat the kind of bowing that was required. Even the older women were made to squat because they could not bow as low as the rules forced them to follow what were due the invaders who set the rules.

On the third day of the armed forces' occupation of our neighborhood, Papa and I fell in line with other residents who were not acquainted with following bowing instructions. Papa who was always dressed according to factors governed by the weather, was attired in his usual coat and tie, thick enough to ward off the December cold.

I was just behind Papa when he started to bow. As he finished the ritual, he tried to resume his walking stride a few steps away, when the sentry shouted at him. Papa was not aware he was the cause of the loud shout. So he stood straight. Then, in a minute, the sentry rushed into Papa, equipped with a whip that was meant for large beasts. The whip landed on Papa several times when he tried to avoid the impact of each blow. Then, when Papa fell, the sentry disrobed Papa. Throwing his coat, tie and heavy pants into a large trash can, the sentry seemed satisfied to see that Papa did not contradict him. Papa was left in his undergarments, tears falling, not just caused by the physical pains, but worried about how to proceed next. He had hoped I would not be given the same harsh treatment since I was only a child.

Then, Papa turned to me. "Go as soon as you can, immediately. Enroll at the Japanese Language School across from the Burnham Park athletic field." I heard Papa's instructions. But I could not leave him without the right clothing. I ran back to our house to get a shirt and pants. I could not dare leave him in his attire which, to my childish mind, was unlike what I knew of him. I had never seen Papa reduced to that heartbreaking state. I joined him in great hopes, tears accompanying my gait, that he could walk back to our house. As soon as he could, he gave me enough funds to enable me to enroll at the aforementioned school.

Returning to our house, I did not leave home until I could follow his instructions to apply liniments to apply on his sore body. He asked for a pitcher of water which he consumed immediately. He was so upset. I looked at Papa. He repeated that I go immediately to the Japanese Language School. He told me that nobody would ever understand commands until translations could be availed of. He said the reason why he was beaten up was because there was no explanation about bowing and how pedestrians could not proceed unless they were cleared to go.

If only even simple communication in English would have surfaced, no beatings would ever have taken place, was his immediate commentary relevant to the very commands he and other pedestrians were made to suffer. Instantly, he was certain it was the deplorable lack of oral communication that was responsible behind the whippings of pedestrians who were at a loss when it came to comprehension of the bowing requirement.

Papa, through his legal background (having served as a justice of the peace in his Ilocos Sur birthplace), clung to his initial reaction attributed to the cruel moves by the sentries who, in their position of command, forced pedestrians to comply with whatever they had in mind, but failed to demonstrate their meaning.

Comprehension of the tools of communication should have taken place and no pedestrians would have been coerced to follow the Japanese military's concept of recognizing authority, was Papa's dictum to all of us, his family.

Not one of our house helpers then and there, wanted to be within the range of the sentries. They begged to stay indoors. They had seen Papa's deplorable state when he just arrived through the house's gates as he continued to shiver continuously while liniments and ice bags had to take care of his pain. He told my mother it wasn't so much the physical pain, but the internal pain he had to suffer in the face of the lack of communication. Mama cried silently as she directed the kitchen help to prepare easy-to-swallow recipes. All of us, their four children, could not help but be moved by Mama's tears. She could not speak at all, but hugged us all to join her in prayer.

In order to make it possible for as many members of our family and our household to communicate with the sentries, Papa underscored how we must learn simple greetings, all stated in the Japanese language. To study the latter, I immediately decided to obey my father, convincing myself to go to the Japanese Language School. He strongly insisted that the enemy's language had to be part of our lives. He stressed how communication would be carried on since the sentries did not converse with pedestrians. All that came from them were shouts accompanied by actions that were not at all explained.

As soon as I was able to leave Papa at home as he nursed his pains from the beatings he received, I soon found my way to the Japanese Language School. I enrolled immediately as soon as I reached the building. I learned about schedules. The would-be students would attend a class of 15 only, the maximum number dictated by the principal. He stressed how the process of elimination would prevail. All members of the newly-announced class would be tested each week; those who could not meet the spoken word's standards and the writing would not be allowed to remain. What each enrollee was supposed to remember acutely about the class was to maintain a serious mien and individual progress was to be noted accordingly by the teacher.

There was one piece of news that we, the high school youngsters clung to: The encouraging facet that liberation forces would be arriving to free us from the enemy. News dailies were not available. In the midst of our ceaseless hopes, we relied on news derived from short-wave radios that a few of our elders kept as secrets. One of the news reports we received was how General Douglas MacArthur who was in Manila when Pearl Harbor, Hawaii was bombed, left for another command. Before he did, he was heard to say "I shall return." It was the latter, a three-word pledge that was a MacArthur original that was passed on among our elders who reminded us every so often how that indelible promise was anchored on freedom and liberty in reference to the re-emergence of troops led by American forces and how peace would return.

What I distinctly recall was the absence of newspapers and publications we were accustomed to read before December 8, 1941. Our social science classes in high school introduced us to the meaning and practice of freedom. We knew it was lost the moment we saw how enemy forces arrived and installed their own barracks.

We were made aware that freedom of the press was truly absent. Democratic institutions which belonged to the Commonwealth government were no longer around, per radio news reports. Totally lost was freedom of expression. Nobody was allowed to talk against the "reigning" forces from the 'land of the rising sun,' during the entire period of enemy occupation. Short-wave radio broadcasts were the sole sources of news done in utmost secrecy.

Information reached my parents about how some of their close friends had joined the guerilla movement. Papa would tell Mama how some of their friends perished as leaders in the movement. Those who outlived the debacle would visit my parents to provide them with the latest reports, in a very hushed manner because the enemy units were still active as they moved around our neighborhood.

Our parents would lead us in prayer as often as they could. When news reports came via short-wave radio, Mama and Papa would share them with us. I was assigned to look out for those who could be eaves-droppers around our compound. Nobody else but the construction workers and our family had any knowledge of our air-raid shelter.

Everyone in our city had to depend on walking. Businesses did not include gas stations. All means of transportation were confiscated by the occupation forces. When I was positive that our family needed only one car, I requested the Japanese soldier moving around our neighborhood, to allow us to keep one car in our garage. He did not object, as long as we could not make use of it at all. That was my very first request articulated in Japanese.

Numbers among us learned how to move fast, not only just walk. We ran too. We had to be punctual at the language school or we would run the risk of being booted out in line with the rigid rules of attendance.

Each day on return from the Japanese Language School, I was able to state known greetings to the sentries who would smilingly acknowledge some few conversational phrases with them.

There was but one type of dressing our parents insisted us to wear:

coveralls. Later, we knew the reason behind their decision. The attire presented the great assist needed to walk or run fast enough in the event of emergencies.

Thankfully, the once foreign language to us became easier to learn after our daily classes. Our mentor was the school's principal who refused to utter even a few words in English. Youth has its pluses. We maintained the classroom discipline that was a constant reminder of our language school's Rules and Regulations handbook, the sole pamphlet in English. We had to commit the latter to memory.

In a six-week period, as students, we had learned basic conversational language in Japanese including their correct usage.

We were taught how to write the **Katakana**, the Japanese basic alphabet. Owing to the fact that I was the sole one from my neighborhood who was an attendee of the language school, I helped my neighbors who needed their individual badges written in Japanese katakana. All civilians had to wear a badge: basic individual badges written in katakana: the name and age, all on a white background for immediate contrast, meant for easy reading.

After an eight-week attendance at school, I was given a story to memorize. Its main characters depicted an elderly couple who relied on their usual everyday needs. My teacher told me to commit the entire story to memory, replete with accompanying gestures. I did follow what I was instructed to do.

To date, I can still remember how the story, a known legend in Japanese childhood literature, stood out. **"Mukashi, mukashi aru tokoro ni odiisang to obasang ga narimasta."**

The legend, adjudged to be popular, detailed how an infant (a boy) was found by the riverside, inside a large peach by an elderly couple who were childless. How the duo saved him alive strengthened their hopes for a child they would raise as their own. The story achieved popularity.

When I memorized the details, my language teacher made me part of his school courses in story-telling. He trained me how to narrate the legend and guided me correctly in the accepted manner of narrating stories. Accompanying the narration included the corresponding gestures in detail.

Not long after, in mid-1943, the city's school system was declared open with the consent of the Japanese-run officials. To keep up with class placement, our class was given examinations to hurdle. I considered myself fortunate enough to qualify for advanced classes. I was instructed to join a senior high school class that underscored the Japanese language as a major part of the curriculum. One distinct change in class assignment came about. Boys and girls no longer shared the same classroom. There was a different side of the building for each separate class based on gender enrollment. I considered it my good fortune to have enrolled in the Japanese Language School, much earlier than my classmates who were to commence with the same beginning classes that I found myself in when I was first introduced to the Japanese language. I was able to attend to other courses required by the academic curricula of senior students growing out of my having learned Japanese ahead of my classmates. They were just starting to learn simple greetings.

I was exuberant when our regular high school class received its first report card of the school year in late 1943. It was the very first time I had seen the rating of 100% appear on my very card. Unsure of the perfect rating's appearance, I asked our head teacher on what appeared on my card. She attributed it to my grade in the Japanese language and my behavior, categorized as deportment.

Evidently, there arose a friendly atmosphere between the Japanese officials and our Baguio city government. It seemed like war wasn't on because rules of travel were no longer as strict as they were disseminated originally. The number of sentries close to our neighborhood was reduced: they were moved to the more crowded areas where retail stores and small market stalls stood by and simple restaurant fare was likewise availed of.

In very early 1944, our high school was invited to an oratorical contest in strict usage of the Japanese language to be held outside Baguio. All members of the Ilocos regional high schools were to assemble in San Fernando, La Union, one of the provincial capitals centrally located in the Ilocos region.

Humbly, I was chosen to represent our high school by the process of elimination among eight (8) contestants who were members of the graduating class.

The Japanese language instructor from whom I had my very first lessons in Japanese volunteered to train me, particularly how to express myself in the manner that would draw keen competition from other provincial capital competitors. He informed me how happy he was when I was selected immediately apart from other contestants meant to represent my high school in a regional competition.

All of us from our respective Ilocos region schools affiliated with the aforesaid contest were informed that we would be provided with comfortable transportation facilities, not just through buses, but cars that belonged to the Japanese officials. They were getting to be cordial as they gradually started to learn how the civilian population responded to rules and regulations imposed by their very rigid instructions.

San Fernando, was indeed a well-known provincial capital that had served earlier during pre-war days as host to many competitive educational contests. Its facilities were scarcely touched by the war. The contest was scheduled in June 1944, shortly before our high school graduation in August that same year.

Off to San Fernando, our delegation went. It seemed like it was a return to the pre-war era. All guests from various capitals of the Ilocos region were on the receiving end of hospitality from the government officials of San Fernando. It did appear as all attendees pertinent to the contest seemed gladdened to get to know one another.

What struck us as youngsters was how the picture of war was never mentioned. We loved talking about our respective high schools: how we all loved representing our home areas was a common theme. We were enjoying our initial meetings with several representatives from our region who did not hesitate to bring with them the delectable sweets that identified their provinces.

Humbly, I was just one of the two girl representatives coming from competitive-ranking high schools. There were nine contestants who delivered the very same, exact piece. We were all of the opinion that all was fair in love and war. Besides, each speaker was judged by the manner of presentation. Stage presence that lent anticipated expression in the same language was underscored by the rules read to the audience as well. There were noted strengths from each speaker. Since each candidate didn't have their own special cheering squad, applause came from all members of the audience which delighted all student speakers who were hoping their time on the stage would be over soon.

The contest judges were all Japanese language educators who came from other locales who were not acquainted at all with any of their contemporaries from other schools. The bottom line, explained to all of us contestants, was one of fairness. Not a single judge knew any contestant at all. Judges didn't know anything about each speaker who was just identified by number.

Of course, the manner of delivery of the same piece was the main criterion in terms of who would emerge winner, according to the head judge who read the rules very clearly.

The contest's conclusion was reached punctually. The judges retreated to a room where it took them a good hour and a half before they all came out singly as they returned to their seats.

Far from bragging, I was unanimously chosen: first-prize winner.

The other two were awarded second prize and honorable mention positions. At first, the judges called the last two prizes before they called my name, the representative of Baguio City High School. The two other awardees were boys from other provincial points.

My school delegation joined me in animation as I was called on the stage to receive my medal and the floral bouquet from the provincial governor who was accompanied by other members of his official group who presented their congratulatory wishes in the form of mementoes from their province. I could not fully hold all the prizes that came with the award. It seemed like a dream for a tiny teenager to enable her to carry all the gifts that went in running away with the premier prize.

What saddened me was the absence of my immediate family members. Of course, from the start, we were informed how not a single one among all the contestants had their parents nor close family relations at the same event. But we didn't realize as youngsters how much we missed our family in the midst of the competition.

A reception was held for all participants and their school representatives. Traditionally, congratulations came from the provincial hosts. Truly, I had missed my parents and siblings who would have loved to witness the competition and a visit to San Fernando, the birthplace of my sole brother.

Returning to my high school the next day, I was greatly surprised to be welcomed by the student body and the faculty at a brief opening program. I was asked to deliver the same winning piece to the delight of my schoolmates who lost no time in greeting me with floral arrangements.

School life beckoned immediately. As seniors, we were given instructions to prepare for our finals. Graduation rites were to follow. Again, there were two graduating classes which denoted separate commencement dates for girls and boys.

My parents received information from guerillas who were disguised as they visited our home. They told Mama and Papa how more and more molestations were committed by the Japanese soldiers who weren't moving in groups any longer. Numbers of the enemy forces had changed to civilian wear. Guessing the enemy's drastic change into civilian attire was easily explained by the guerillas who described how the enemy could not clearly be identified away from their uniforms. Switching to civilian garb, away from their organizational units, seemed to achieve the desired effect; from a distance, it was difficult to distinguish them.

Meanwhile, through guarded information, my parents received

word how General MacArthur had just walked ashore on October 20, 1944, as soon as the U.S. forces he commanded landed at Palo, Leyte, some ten (10) miles south of Tacloban City, in the Visayas. That word about the MacArthur return became so inspirational. It was repeated over the radio. How that all-important event caught the entire country on fire was beyond word. Each time we turned to listen to secret broadcasts, we heard the news over and over again. It was a clear signal that peace was foreseen.

Word spread through every medium possible. The underground units caught the first salvo was reported. The population of Northern Luzon awaited word most anxiously as similar landings were moving in various parts of the country. Papa listened to the Lingayen Gulf landing. The latter event proved there was scarcely any doubt in any Filipino's mind that the promise of General MacArthur to "return" moved closer and closer to fulfillment.

Baguio, as described by those who walked through the hills and mountains, spoke of the valor of the guerilla units who made safety possible for civilians who were on foot, returned home unscathed.

Christmas came. All we could do in remembrance of that most-loved holiday was to sing the melodies in English that described the happiness and joy in awaiting the arrival of the Christ Child. We did not display the ornaments needed for Christmas tree decorations. They were tucked safely in our house's ceiling, all over the building we called home for the longest time.

Papa was able to bring chocolate candies and a few home-baked goods available from a few groceries nearby. Meanwhile, although mail service was long disrupted, our family received hand-delivered greeting cards away from Baguio, from relatives who did not hide their longing to see a termination of the war.

Unfortunately, four days after Christmas, I was feeling very sick. It was something I had never felt at all since I started my life as a teenager. I was rocked by incessant aches all over. I was in so much pain that my father had to go by foot to the residence of our family doctor, Ernesto Abellera, M.D., close to the start of a new date, the 29th of December, one of the last days of 1944, so he could inform the doctor as fast as possible. In an hour and a half, Papa arrived with Dr. Abellera. He asked several questions. But I could not provide the right answers except by shaking my head and nodding when his queries drew the fitting answers.

After close to a two-hour session, the good doctor diagnosed my case as one caused by "appendix problems." He strongly advised how I had to be rushed to the emergency room of the Notre Dame Hospital, so many kilometers away. Papa was fearful that I would become so ill. He approached one of the sentries in the neighborhood (who spoke and understood English) and had a small, unmarked armored car. Papa asked him to take the three of us to the hospital. In a few minutes, the doctor, Papa and myself found ourselves headed to the hospital. I talked to the soldier in Japanese so haltingly that he was surprised I could still talk. He asked me how I learned Japanese since I was but a child. He returned my comments in his language and expressed his curiosity about how I learned their very medium of expression since I was "still young." He continued to inquire: "How do you regard Japanese as a language when you were trained in English?" I told him how my father encouraged me to attend the Japanese Language School and how I found the language so interesting to learn **katakana** too, as well as **hiragana** later.

As soon as I was "delivered" to the hospital, I proceeded to thank my benefactor whom I found out to be Catholic, as he read the hospital's name: Notre Dame, and I pronounced it the way we were taught: in French. He softly informed me in correct English that his parents were in California. I thanked him in his native tongue, but he replied to me in an unaccented manner, "You are most welcome, miss."

After laboratory procedures' results were out, I was scheduled for the surgery that was to take place in a few days' time.

Dr. Abellera called my case "good morning appendix," because as soon as the incision was made, the surgery was ready for the entire process. I was returned to my room. With the almost unbearable pain gone, my speech was no longer disabled. I asked one of the nurses to request a priest to talk to me. One came after a half-hour wait. I asked for the priestly blessing and confession.

Likewise, I requested to be given extreme unction which I received. It made me so thankful and grateful that I was still alive to think of the blessings that were to be anticipated before one's exit from this terrestrial globe.

I looked at the calendar. It was the 6th day of January 1945, the known feast day of the Three Kings. I inquired from the doctor how long I would be expected to recover, to be back to my old walking self. He had one response: "Patience."

Doctor Abellera was frank enough to advise me to take my time to recover because I wasn't just physically tested, but emotionally too; I had confided in him how I would be facing death while a war was still going on, and would no longer be around with my siblings and parents were peace to be returned to the country.

After a week in bed, I asked Chita, the nurse, to help me get up so I could go to the chapel across my room. She understood my wishes, but jokingly stated that I be attired in the proper outfit.

It was a few steps to the chapel. I managed to walk alone. All of a sudden, my tears of gratitude in acquiring a new lease on life came to the fore. I was able to get on my knees and finished my rosary then and there without assistance in getting up. Again, I was in tears. I was very thankful. I couldn't keep my tears away. Before long, I was sobbing and wondering how the rest of my family were. I had not seen them for the longest time. It was too much to ask them to visit me owing to the distance they had to traverse by foot. Three weeks' absence from home was evaluated in years.

The kind nurse who just stood by, was crying very softly. After we left the chapel, she informed me how she noticed my thankfulness as a recovering patient. Her comments were appreciative from having observed a child's gratitude. She added how I was able to remain as a well-behaved patient without any complaint aired at all.

Chita asked me to continue praying because my time to be released wouldn't be that soon. There would be more tests to follow. I accepted her broad hint without question. I asked for a calendar. It seemed I was not aware that it was my 16th day in the hospital. I could still hear the sounds of war: bombings had stopped; but a new sound was being heard.

I was notified it was called artillery shelling. The bombings ceased completely. Artillery shelling arrived frequently, all its sounds heard before darkness would set in. Evenings turned quiet. But lights had to be replaced by candlelight. The use of lamps was made to the minimum.

When my fourth week of hospitalization arrived, I was accompanied by an attendant to move around my same floor, but cautioned not to make it up and down the length of the stairway since elevator service had been halted a long time ago. Chita warned me to take but a few steps because having lain in bed that long was enough to cause dizzy spells, no matter how brief walks would be.

I was more than thankful how I had the energy to walk around. Moving about although via slow motion, contributed to my pent-up wish to return home. I was extremely homesick. Alone, I cried myself to sleep.

Thankfully, our house was spared by bombing or the artillery shelling. Drinking water from the spring in our yard was nature's gift. I did look forward to the spring water because I drank boiled water at the hospital.

I was to return home to our Ferguson Road family home from the hospital on February 10th. Of course, I could not negotiate the lengthy distance from the Notre Dame Hospital area to reach home by foot.

Papa thought of something that would be of immeasurable help to me in my weakened state. He lost no time in contacting my Japanese language teacher, Mr. Tachibana, who was still in his residence's office. Quickly, Papa informed me how he was able to reach my teacher and how he explained my physical disability. In a two-hour period, an armored car was on the hospital grounds. After my father received my discharge papers, he led my teacher to my room. My teacher greeted me generously in Japanese. He informed me he was happy that I had not forgotten how the language became a principal phase of my life.

I told Mr. Tachibana how I had not forgotten his instructions at all.

He said: "Nippongo wa, Ajiya no kotoba desu." Of course, I added how the language I learned from him became a principal phase of my wartime education, not only as presented by book knowledge, but practical use of conversation, and the etiquette that accompanied speech.

In a short period, we were home, as we continued to converse in the language he had taught me. My father joined me in thanking Mr. Tachibana profusely. Quietly, my teacher told Papa how he was an officer of the Japanese military. Papa did not ask him any questions at all.

My neighborhood that had not seen an armored car in the company of Japanese military dressed in their full and complete uniform started to fear how an invasion of our family home was about to ensue. I got out of the vehicle, talked to a few of my older neighbors who had gathered to protect me with their blankets and umbrellas. I informed them it was not that necessary to entertain any fears at all. I explained to them what the presence of the Japanese in military attire had signified.

Hurriedly, I told my well-meaning neighbors that the Japanese officer was my old language teacher whose assistance was vital in fetching me from the hospital. As fast as I could, I related to them how I would not have made it back home that same day when slow steps had to be made every so often, after half-a-mile, at the longest, because I had lost so much strength. It would have taken me more than two days to get home had I walked.

My neighbors ran to my teacher and thanked him profusely in English. They were so teary-eyed as they joyfully stated in one of the few greetings I had taught them to say: "Arigato Gozaimasu."

I reiterated my thankfulness to my teacher. He never, never spoke with me away from the language he had taught me. I inquired about his wife and their two daughters who became my friends when I was attending the language school. He just smiled when he told me they were "home." It turned out that he meant they were back in

Japan. Informing me further, Mr. Tachibana said how he was all by himself, and his men as they were ready to "serve their country." He bade me "sayonara," after he had seen me back home, back to my mother and my siblings. I expressed my family's gratitude to him. He left me a piece of paper which had an address of Mrs. Tachibana and their two daughters whom he described as having joined a few families who were returned to their original home in Japan.

Quietly, my old teacher gave me a piece of advice. "Apply for a scholarship in Japan where you can teach English." He did sound off as though war was going to end soon and all would be well with the world.

As my concerned neighbors started to leave the scene, I was convinced they were being extra-cautious. They felt certain that the presence of Japanese in their military wear was trouble enough. They did not leave until Mr. Tachibana and his armored car left the premises. They lingered around our front yard as they asked me for the correct pronunciation of certain greetings in Japanese. Basic queries surfaced: "Ikaga desu ka? Isogashi desu ne?"

The period spent with my neighbors who reacted to seeing the Japanese military was an illustration of an immediate need when every facet of living in a war-torn country required exact elucidation that could easily have been mistaken for a misunderstanding of enormity: how an inadequacy of a foreign language could redound to a herculean case of erroneous conclusions.

Papa mentioned how he overheard conversational exchanges in Japanese between my teacher and myself when we were homeward-bound. He was hugely surprised to listen to me as I spoke Japanese, not as a stranger to the language, but as one who was "at home" using a foreign tongue. It was the lengthy drive that gave my father the opportunity to listen to the entire conversation between my Japanese teacher and myself.

After weeks of staying in our main house, I knew I was gathering strength. I learned how Mama was able to procure food. She informed me how barter took place at times: how our fruits and vegetables would be exchanged for chicken and beef pieces. Providentially, our rice supply lasted long. Papa was correct in his earlier thinking when he resorted to storing numbers of rice sacks in our house. He was able to trade rice with whatever the nuns at the Holy Family College would spare. We were gladdened to see refined sugar bartered with our rice. When combined, the two products were tasty enough to see them converted to rice cakes.

Since the air-raid strikes were no longer around, the family had less use of the shelter during the day. However safe it looked, my parents still wanted us to seek shelter because of the unabated artillery shelling, particularly during the day. Papa likewise wanted us to be together when evening arrived.

Lita, the oldest among my siblings, continued to hear daily mass at times at the nearby church when the artillery shelling would stop. One day, she wanted to see whether or not some of our closest neighbors had returned to their homes. She convinced my brother and a younger sister to join her as she did wish to welcome our neighbors who had gone to evacuation centers early enough during the arrival of the initial bombings.

Reportedly, the three of them went to our neighbor's garage because they saw their huge garage door was wide open. Fright was theirs when they encountered a fully-armed Japanese member of the military. He stopped them in their tracks. Nobody was allowed to move. He commanded them to raise their hands.

My younger sister (then 9 years old) was immediately struck with fear. In the few words she knew Japanese, "kyodai," she informed the soldier she had a sister, as she pointed toward our house. The armed Japanese soldier, in an angry tone commanded my older sister (then, a 19-year old) to kneel in front of him, as though he was ready to chop her head with his sword. My brother, a 14-year old, had remembered a few Japanese words, "nesang, nesang, Nipongo," as he tearfully told the soldier how he had another older sister who spoke Japanese. In fact, my younger sister had already ran to our air-raid shelter as she was sobbing loudly in her efforts to notify me about the incident that befell them.

I responded as fast as I could walk to get to the scene that was taking place. Lita was likewise sobbing loudly in hysterics, as she was still in the same kneeling position described to me hastily by my sister. Lita was reciting her "last prayers." I hastened to speak to the Japanese military who was in front of Lita. He questioned me as fast as he could.

"Why didn't your family leave the city for evacuation centers at least twenty (20) kilometers away?" Speaking to me in Japanese after I greeted him, he talked very rapidly as though he was in a hurry to leave. I told him how I was hospitalized; how I had to undergo an emergency surgery; how I was able to leave the hospital for home, thanks to my Japanese language teacher.

The soldier seemed impressed that I could respond to him in Japanese. Then, he started to introduce himself. He informed me that he was an officer of his country's naval forces. He immediately apologized for having detained my siblings. Then he asked in a strong voice why we were the only Filipinos he had seen in the neighborhood after he made a three-day reconnaissance of the area.

Continuing his quest for answers to his questions, he asked me how I knew Japanese. I informed him how I had close to a 4-year tutelage of the language, and how I happened to have met the commanding officer of the area: General Nagasaki, who came to our residence to deliver his congratulatory message and present when I won the regional prize in a Northern Luzon competition.

In the process, the soldier released my siblings who waited for me. He likewise inquired why our family did not join other evacuee groups whom he had noted while he was abandoned by some of his men. He did not hesitate to let me know how American forces were closing in our city. I informed him without hesitation that I was recently hospitalized. Then and there, as he looked at his watch, he informed me that he knew English well. Still in Japanese, he said he was sorry my siblings were confronted and so frightened by him.

Still apologetic, the soldier said: "Shitsurei shimasta, gomen nasai." He was sorry he frightened my siblings, as he took off his cap. He started to speak in English, loud enough for my siblings to hear him. I complimented him on his knowledge of English. He returned to speaking further in Japanese, how he had lived in America for twelve (12) years; was recruited in the midst of his college education, based on his communication skills in both Japanese and English. I immediately asked his permission to allow my siblings to join me. In front of all of us, he introduced himself, gave his rank as an officer, and told us his name: "Buma Sang." Slowly, but loud enough for us to hear him, he informed us how American forces would be arriving in our area "within hours." If we wanted to be spared from a house-to-house fight, he advised that our entire household should leave the area as fast as possible.

"Seeking shelter at least thirty (30) miles away should be your next action," he emphasized.

Hearing from the Japanese soldier was indeed the very first time we heard that liberation could truly be that close. It confirmed what Papa had heard over the short-wave radio: How, in thirty-two (32) hours, Baguio would be at the vortex of liberation forces, and how the Japanese holdouts were leaving frantically for the mountains near us.

The four of us scampered as fast as we could to our air-raid shelter, which, for all of us, stood strong and firm in the midst of our fears.

I joined my parents immediately as we were comforted by seeing everyone together. As we said our thanksgiving and gratitude in knowing that all of us were completely in one place, we recounted to our parents how one single incident that almost cost my siblings' lives could have ensued: we joined each other in prayer.

It was still early, very early 1945. Word had spread around that the war had ended. Liberation forces started to arrive. Allied tanks and bulldozers occupied the main roads as fast as daylight appeared. Those who lived close to the highways went around to spread the message of immeasurable cheer and gratitude that our liberators had finally arrived. No enemy forces were seen at all. They seemed to have completely disappeared from sight.

We were spared house-to-house combat fighting. The populace cheered when the allied troops started to set up their Quonset huts to serve as their living quarters and offices at the same time. The "liberators" as the population called the allied forces, were greatly surprised to converse with us in English. Initially, they were speaking very slowly. But when they heard English spoken by the curious youngsters who milled around them, they proceeded to converse with everyone in English.

Children gathered around the American soldiers who were letting the children reach out for such goodies as Hershey's and Babe Ruth chocolates. Housewives had their share of canned fruits and jars of vegetables, cereals and other goodies.

Most of the former Baguio residents who had left their homes started to return. Although electric power was not restored immediately, great cheer was symbolized to see lighted fireplaces and floral pots that had pine tree seedlings, our city's trademark. Of course, the bomb-hit surroundings were easily identified: all hard-to-miss, sadly marked by their state: in rubble and ruin. Yet, the morale sparked by the truth of liberation was stronger than the lack of facilities. Patience had to be the premier name of the next life for large numbers of the populace who became survivors of World War II, profoundly stated in their own belief in prayer and justice.

As year 1945 was drawing to a close, the civilian population of Baguio was slowly returning to what was termed "normalcy."

My parents commenced their planning on my return to the pathway of education. They had no other choice but for me to enroll at their same alma mater, the University of the Philippines (U. P.) in Manila. At first, I let them know what I knew in terms of the vicissitudes of schooling in formerly war-torn Manila: how trying it would be amid the intense heat; dust; lack of accessible transportation; the type of boarding facilities students would find; high costs of everything: books; school supplies and the like to meet college requirements.

But Mama and Papa had firmly resolved that I should start my college education immediately. They had January 1946 firmly in mind. The college of Liberal Arts and Sciences of the U.P. had re-opened its doors in July of 1945; the second semester was to follow in January 1946. Buildings were scarred and joined the sorry plight of war-torn casualties that indicated how the Battle of Manila took place: heavy door-to-door shooting and burned areas told their tales of woe and loss of life.

My parents looked for a dormitory close to the newly-opened U.P. on Padre Faura Street, Manila. The boarding fee appeared far from affordable; but Mama and Papa saw the pluses. I could just walk back and forth to the college. There were two small restaurants close to the dormitory likewise. I would be able to benefit from their offerings at any given time. Their business hours coincided with our free school schedules.

The same restaurants served hamburgers and sandwiches which we boarders welcomed accordingly. Our dormitory kitchen was merely open just for breakfast and a light supper.

Oh yes, we found ourselves going for ice cream and sliced cakes. We were getting very tired of the usual dormitory menus; the presence of the Fairmont Restaurant on Taft Avenue, Manila, was a godsend to us. Our confidence grew as we were assured we would never go hungry as long as the restaurant would stay open.

The registration process at the University was clear enough. I filled up all the necessary information papers since I had already submitted my high school transcripts to the University Registrar's Office as soon as I arrived in Manila from Baguio.

Much later, long after college graduation took place, I made a visit to our University Library. I looked at an index of war stories. I noted one that zeroed in on articles underscoring the joint forces that made victory in our homeland reality; how crucial it was to the cause of the Allied Forces to see the return of Baguio and to see the ultimate defeat of the enemy. It was part of the many histories of war. It made me very sad when I remembered the dates of that very early 1945 campaign.

I learned how the essence of caring can go very far. The much-heard "through thick and thin" is truly relevant when one clings on a mission to remain alive and well. My friendship with my Japanese language teacher and his family had served me in good stead.

The aforementioned amity opened so many doors of comprehension of mankind for me, a child of war. The four-year occupation of the Philippines' enemy proved how a trying era endeared itself.

When one's life chapters continue to remain as virtual reminders that there is one resounding goodness in how a human being's concern for others rises above all other factors, life becomes indescribably precious. Experiences gained from strife lead the way. Goodness tends to merge naturally bereft of hate, against the backdrop of a war whose conclusion was unknown, cannot be taken for granted. Only time would be able to foretell what had to ensue.

My father, as the head of our family did what he could muster under those trying circumstances.

I have become a firm believer that one cannot manufacture traits. Nor virtues. They come from the heart. Through my exposure to humanity, I have learned so much. There is still so much to seek: So many pursuits to follow as leads continue to appear in the name of peace for all mankind.

Goodness cannot be measured in terms of the tangible. The latter will not live forever. It is the intangible that will continue to persist just like time itself. I found out how my father's love for his family came naturally as his faith in God guided him during war and peace.

Going back to those trying scenes, Papa had to deal with, is an indicator that one cannot shirk responsibilities.

As I conclude, I pray war will never come to this country, the adopted land I chose to continue to call home for close to six decades.

The very early lessons I learned from World War II are constantly enshrined in my memory. They are not learned from books. Gradually, they come from experience and common sense laced with reality.

War can never be defined accurately.

Each survivor has her/his original version to tell the world.

But there's a single, solitary lesson that war is meant to announce to the world-at-large. Truth and courage have their singular roles to fulfill as life goes on. Love is timeless in war and in peace as learned from my father who made fast and wise decisions. He not only infused courage in us. But he passed on what he himself had learned: war and peace are similar in their ends. Love is direly needed in war. It is thus underscored in peace. Both factors need to navigate via the same factors when trying situations arise and their very solutions can be resorted to.

One's loving and caring self will continue to exist beyond life itself because the generations after will keep their vows to hold on, preserved unwittingly by the memory of their forebears, as time goes on.

How certain realities surface, made possible through the dissemination of the written word have made their niche in history. It is no longer going to be treated as trivial. Its place in life will continue to live on as remembrances are attributed to the heart, grace and mind. Memories will never be effaced even by time itself. It is the invaluable role of the written word that will be a continuing source of truth that will remain timeless while memories indescribably cling to their respective values as they take their place through the medium of affection and remembrance without end.

As I go down memory lane, as a child, I learned how parenthood cannot be measured by material gains. One learns an unforgettable, unblemished remembrance of how parenthood is shared during both times of conflict and amity. Parents are who they are. They will not shirk any responsibility in bringing up their families despite trying times. They are selfless. They will give what they can as they are able to share what they can offer materially without hurdling their own cares ahead of their families. I am in debt for my parents' devotion who, with their own brand of wisdom and common sense made it possible to survive a world war despite the alien forces that were complete strangers to them.

When it dawned on me that I had not adequately thanked my parents for giving us a new life, I promised them I'd never let them down. As children, we all looked forward to a future which was meant to usher in reality; how we would hurdle the requirements of college education and be able to look forward to leading professional fields of endeavor.

My parents nurtured dreams for all of us: to be able to be worthy citizens of our homeland that suffered a great deal traced to the trauma that World War II had brought. They came to the United States of America as immigrants.

Yet, they were beaming with pride when they saw all five of their children take their place as worthy citizens of a new land, thanks to their aspirations in education that bore fruit.

As a beneficiary of my parents' wisdom and care, I dedicate this book to all parents who have, without any desire or praise, or the slightest wish to be repaid, gave freely of themselves in war and in peace.

A global war can never efface the lessons attributed to the people who have, through no fault of theirs, experienced how they have become daughters and sons of war.

Lourdes Justo Astraquillo (Mrs. Hermie T. Ongkeko), Widow of Colonel Hermie T. Ongkeko, class '51, Philippine Military Academy (Ret. Armed Forces of the Philippines)